Community L   &

3

For Mum – you are wonderful.

First published in 2010
by Hodder Children's Books

Text and illustrations copyright © Michael Broad 2010

Hodder Children's Books
338 Euston Road
London NW1 3BH

Hodder Children's Books Australia
Level 17/207 Kent Street
Sydney NSW 2000

A catalogue record of this book is available from the British Library.

ISBN: 978 0 340 98947 0
10 9 8 7 6 5 4 3 2 1

Printed in China

Hodder Children's Books is a division
of Hachette Children's Books.
An Hachette UK Company
www.hachette.co.uk

Can you spot the blue bird?

Forget*Me*Not
Friendship Blossoms

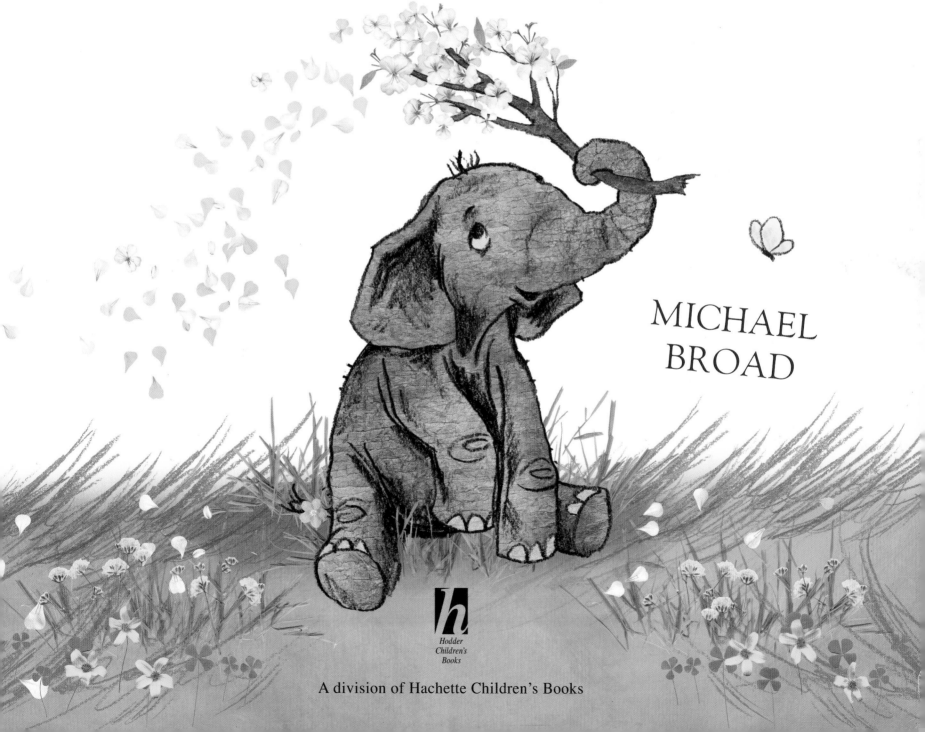

MICHAEL
BROAD

Hodder
Children's
Books

A division of Hachette Children's Books

WHEN THE HERD ARRIVED AT THE WATERING HOLE,
Forget-Me-Not stayed close to his mother.

'There are so many different animals, Mama,' he whispered.
'How will I make friends?'
'Just be yourself,' she smiled.
'They'll soon see how wonderful you are.'

Forget-Me-Not splashed into the water and headed for
the huge hippos.

'Will you be my friends?' he asked.
'I like to wallow in the water too.'

'You're much too small
to wallow with us,'
huffed the hippos, and sank
beneath the surface.

'Will you be my friends?' he asked the lazy lizards,
who were sailing in the sun. 'That looks like lots of fun!'

'You're much too big
    to play with us,'
laughed the lizards, and swiftly sailed away.

Forget-Me-Not approached the other young elephants,
feeling sure that he was almost the right size.

'Will you be my friends?' he asked.
'I'm not too big or too small to play ball.'

'You're too young
            to play with us,'
they said, and turned their backs
on the little elephant.

Before he went to sleep that night,
Forget-Me-Not huddled close to
his mother.

'No one wants to be my friend,
Mama,' he sighed. 'I must not
be wonderful at all.'

'You are, my darling,' she said.
'But friendships sometimes need
time to blossom.'

'What's a blossom?'
asked Forget-Me-Not.

'Blossoms are special flowers that grow on trees,' said his mother. 'They take time to bloom, but are always worth the wait.'

And she stroked his head until he was fast asleep.

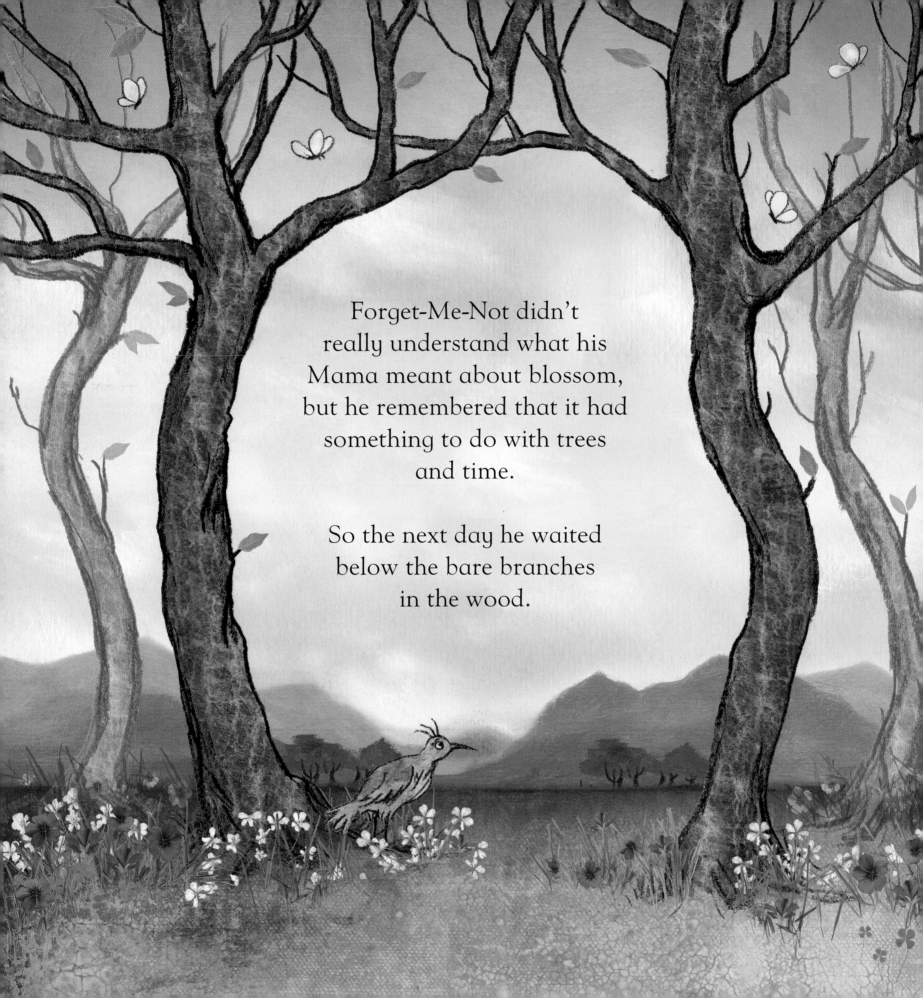

Forget-Me-Not didn't
really understand what his
Mama meant about blossom,
but he remembered that it had
something to do with trees
and time.

So the next day he waited
below the bare branches
in the wood.

He felt very much
alone, until...

'Hello, I'm Cherry,'
said a voice from above.
'What are you doing?'

Forget-Me-Not looked up
to see a young giraffe
peering down at him.

'I'm waiting for
the blossom,' he said.

'Me too,' gasped Cherry.
'My Mama says the blossoms
are beautiful!'

'My Mama says that friendships
blossom,' said Forget-Me-Not.

'I don't see how flowers could
possibly make a friendship,'
Cherry frowned.

Forget-Me-Not and Cherry stood beneath different trees, each waiting for their own particular flowers to arrive.

'Do you want to play while we wait?' asked Cherry.

'OK,' Forget-Me-Not shrugged.

As the days passed by,
Forget-Me-Not and Cherry
spent all of their time together.
They played tag among the
trees and chased butterflies
around the trunks.

Sometimes they simply sat in the shade

and enjoyed each other's company.

One day, the hippos and the
lizards and the elephants
approached them, gazing above
their heads in amazement.

Forget-Me-Not and
Cherry were having so much fun together
they hadn't noticed that the blossom had
bloomed, filling the sky with bright pink flowers!

Everyone wanted to play with
the blossom, but the hippos were
too big and the lizards too lazy,
and like Forget-Me-Not, the young
elephants couldn't stretch their
trunks up that high.

Cherry smiled.
She reached up and
nudged a branch of
blossom, showering
Forget-Me-Not with
tiny pink petals.

He had become a
very special friend.

Forget-Me-Not invited the
other animals to join in their fun
and soon he had lots of friends.
He did not mind at all if they
were bigger, or smaller,
or older than him.

But Cherry was always his
best friend – and like his Mama,
she thought Forget-Me-Not
was wonderful!

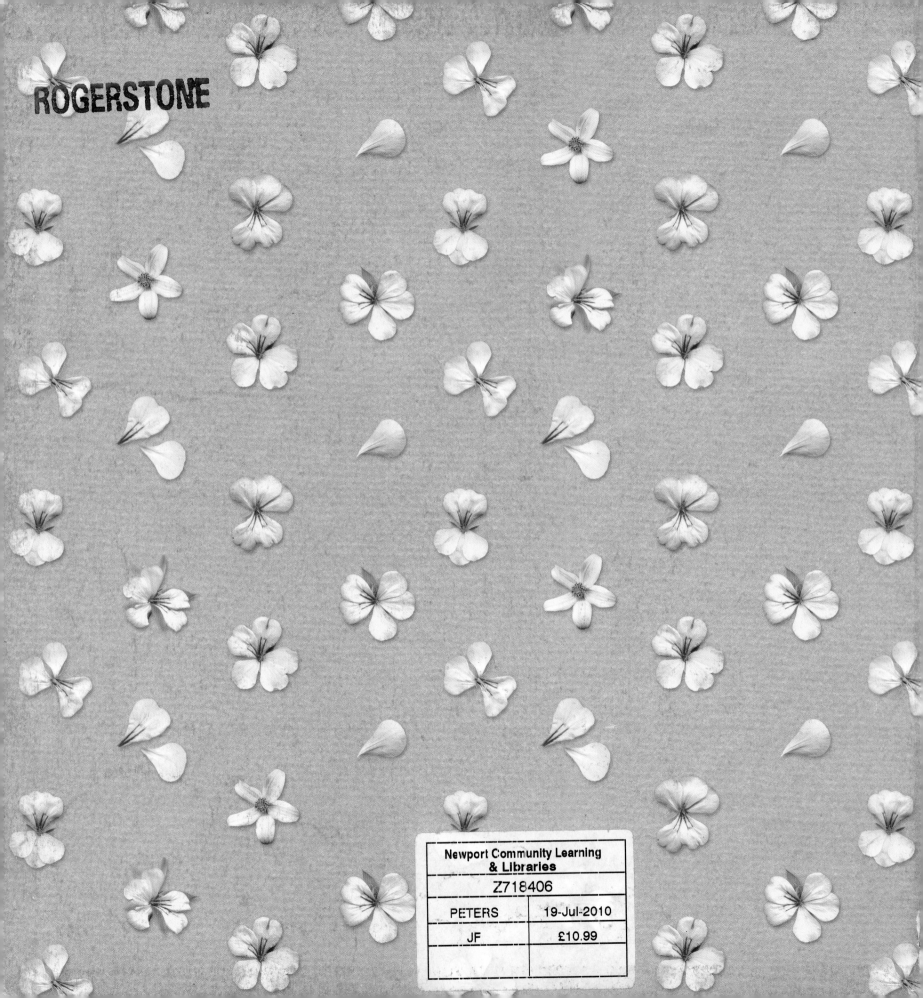

ROGERSTONE